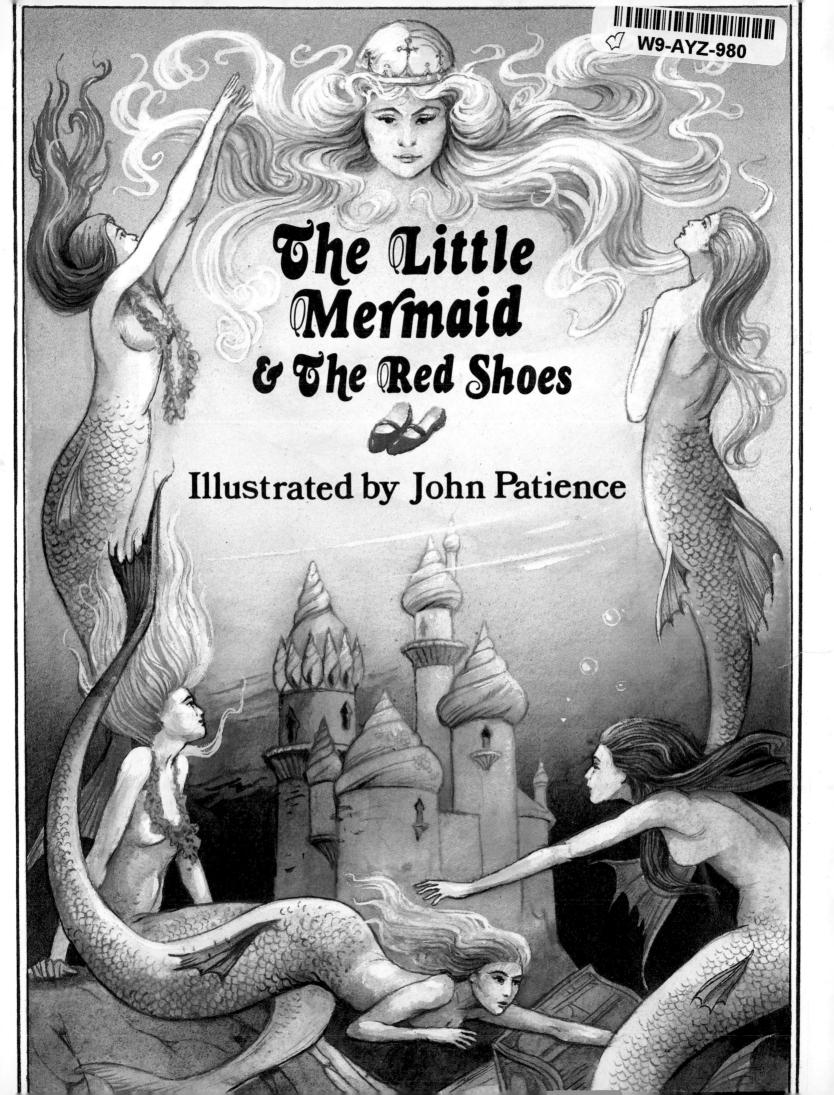

The Little Mermaid
& The Red Shoes

Illustrated by John Patience

W9-AYZ-980

The Little Mermaid

Far, far from land in the deepest waters of the ocean, lived the Mer King. His palace was made of coral and its long pointed windows of amber. The roof was covered with oyster shells and in each one lay a beautiful pearl. The Mer King had been a widower for many years, but his life was brightened by his daughters. These six mermaid Princesses were all very lovely, but the most beautiful of them all was the youngest. Her complexion was as fine as a rose petal and her eyes were as blue as the deepest lake.

Most of all the little mermaid loved to listen to her grandmother telling stories about the world above the sea, about the flowers with wonderful fragrances and the creatures called birds which flew through the trees. "When you are fifteen you will be allowed to swim to the surface and see all these things for yourself," said her grandmother.

So the little mermaid waited as, one by one, her elder sisters went up to see the world above the sea. They returned with tales of cities with twinkling lights, music and the sound of human voices. They were all excited with these things at first, but gradually they grew tired of them and preferred to stay at home in the palace.

At last came the little mermaid's fifteenth birthday. Her grandmother brushed her hair and put a crown upon her head so that everyone would know she was a princess. Then she rose up to the surface.

The sun had just set, the air was warm and the sea was calm. A little way off a great galleon floated upon the water. Its rigging was hung with coloured lights and the sound of music and laughter came from it.

The little mermaid swam close to a cabin window and a wave lifted her up so that she could peep in. They were having a party. It was the Prince's birthday and everyone was enjoying themselves. "The Prince is very handsome," thought the mermaid. After a little while, everyone came up on deck and set off hundreds of fireworks, which burst into beautiful, sparkling colours in the night sky. Then, as the mermaid watched, a storm began to blow up. The waves rose higher and higher, lifting the ship up with them, then crashing it back down again like a tiny toy. The galleon tossed and rolled, creaked and groaned. Then suddenly a wave the size of a mountain fell down upon it. The mast snapped like a reed, the ship rolled over and the next moment it was gone.

The little mermaid searched around in the wreck-age of floating wood for the Prince and at last she found him. He was quite unconscious and half drowned. She took hold of him and kept his head above the waves.

In the morning the little mermaid came upon a bay. She took the Prince and lay him on the dry sand in the warm sun. Then she swam out to sea and waited.

Soon, a girl from a nearby convent came by and discovered the Prince. She called for help and her friends came and carried the Prince away to care for him.

The little mermaid was terribly sad. The Prince would never know she had saved his life. She dived below the waves and returned to her father's palace. But the little mermaid spent more and more of her time thinking about the Prince and began to ask her grandmother lots of questions about the world above

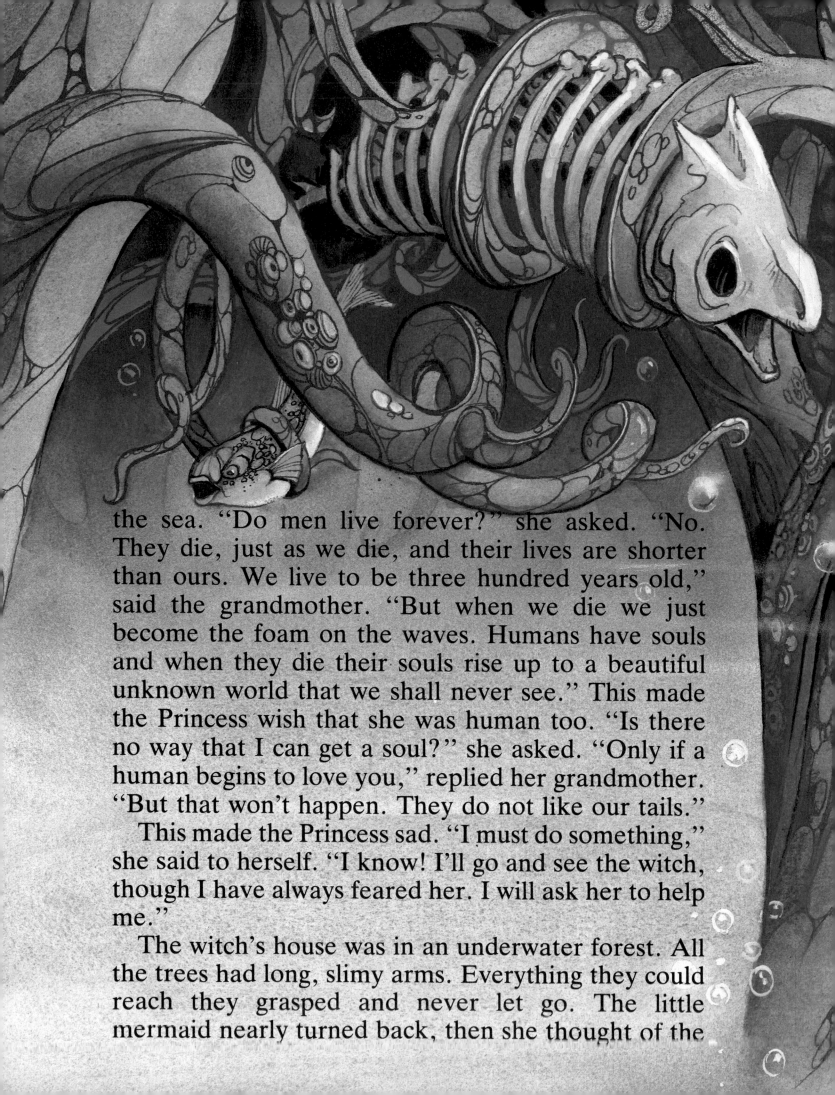

the sea. "Do men live forever?" she asked. "No. They die, just as we die, and their lives are shorter than ours. We live to be three hundred years old," said the grandmother. "But when we die we just become the foam on the waves. Humans have souls and when they die their souls rise up to a beautiful unknown world that we shall never see." This made the Princess wish that she was human too. "Is there no way that I can get a soul?" she asked. "Only if a human begins to love you," replied her grandmother. "But that won't happen. They do not like our tails."

This made the Princess sad. "I must do something," she said to herself. "I know! I'll go and see the witch, though I have always feared her. I will ask her to help me."

The witch's house was in an underwater forest. All the trees had long, slimy arms. Everything they could reach they grasped and never let go. The little mermaid nearly turned back, then she thought of the

handsome Prince again and this gave her courage, so she swam on as fast as she could until she came to the witch's house. It was made of bones. Snails crawled around it and the witch herself sat stroking a large toad. "I know what you have come for," said the witch. "You want legs like humans, instead of your beautiful tail. You are foolish, but I will grant you your wish. You shall have legs and walk and dance upon them as light as a feather. But every time your feet touch the ground it will feel as though you are walking on knives. I will give you a magic potion, but in return you must give me your beautiful voice." "But without a voice, how will I win the Prince?" asked the mermaid. "You must use your lovely eyes and your charm," said the witch.

So the little mermaid agreed to give away her voice and, carrying the witch's potion in a bottle, she swam up to the surface to the Prince's palace. There she sat on the marble steps in the darkness and drank the magic liquid. She felt a dreadful pain as if a sword was

piercing her heart, then she fainted away. When she woke up it was morning. She looked down and saw that her tail had become two slim legs. Standing in front of her was the handsome Prince. He covered her with his cloak and asked her who she was and how she came to be there. She could only smile at him. He led her to the palace and gave her some beautiful clothes to wear. Everyone said how gracefully she walked, and how beautifully she danced. The Prince especially was enchanted and said that she must stay with him forever. The little mermaid was very happy, but all the time her feet hurt just as the sea witch had told her they would.

Each night, when everyone was asleep, the little mermaid crept out of the palace and went to bathe her feet in the sea. One evening her sisters came to visit her and told her how sad they were without her and how much her father and grandmother missed her.

Meanwhile, the Prince had grown very fond of the little mermaid. "You remind me of a girl I once saw," he told her. "My ship was wrecked in a storm. When I woke up a girl had helped me to shore. She is the only person I could ever really love. I am so happy that you remind me of her." This made the little mermaid sad. "He doesn't know that I saved him. He thinks that it was one of the girls from the convent, and they do not marry." But of course she had given her voice to the sea witch and could not tell the Prince the truth.

One day the Prince told her that he was going away on a long journey which his parents had arranged for him. He was to meet a princess in another kingdom who they hoped he might marry. "I shall not love her," he told the little mermaid sadly. "I can only love the girl who saved my life." But when at last the Prince arrived in the foreign kingdom and met the Princess, he was amazed to discover that she was indeed the same girl who he imagined had saved him from drowning. She had been sent to the convent to learn how to be a princess. The little mermaid thought that her heart would break. At the Prince's wedding she walked behind the Princess and carried her train.

That night when it grew dark everyone went on board the ship.

All the coloured lamps were lit and there was dancing and great merriment. It looked just like the party the little mermaid had seen so long ago.

When everyone had gone to bed she stood looking over the ship's rail, out to sea. Suddenly her five sisters appeared. They looked very pale and their long hair had gone. "We have given our hair to the sea witch for this magic knife," they said. "If you kill the Princc with it before the sun rises, you will become a mermaid again."

The little mermaid took the knife and went to where the Prince lay sleeping with his bride, but she found that she could not kill him. Instead she took the knife and threw it into the sea. The waves blazed with coloured light where it landed. Then the little mermaid threw herself into the sea and slowly turned into foam.

As the sun rose, she felt its warmth. She heard sweet voices and saw strange lights in the sky. Then she felt herself being lifted up and soon she was in the sky with the lights all around her. "We are taking you to join the daughters of the air," they said. "Mermaids do not have souls and neither do we, but we can earn our souls by the good deeds we do. We send cool breezes to hot countries to refresh the children. We spread the scent of flowers for everyone to enjoy. If you help us, in three hundred years you will have a soul."

On the ship the Prince and Princess wondered where the beautiful girl who could not speak had gone. Sadly, they looked at the sea as if they guessed that she had thrown herself into the waves. They didn't see the little mermaid wave goodbye as she drifted behind a cloud.

The Red Shoes

There was once a girl named Karen whose mother died when she was very small. An old lady who was riding by in a big old-fashioned carriage saw Karen in the street and felt sorry for her. She decided to adopt her and bring her up as her own daughter.

Karen was dressed in beautiful clothes and taught to read and sew. You would think that she would have been happy, but she became very vain. "I want a pair of red shoes like the ones the Princess wears," said Karen. At first her new mother refused to buy them, but at last she gave in.

"I will wear my new shoes to go to church," said Karen. "Everyone will admire them." Well, I'm afraid that this was a great mistake, because Karen was so busy thinking about her shoes in the church that she completely forgot to say her prayers. As soon as the service was over and Karen stepped out of the church, the red shoes began to dance, all by themselves! They danced and danced and Karen could not take them off.

"Help! Stop me!" she cried, but the red shoes were much too nimble and, try as they might, no-one could catch her. Away she danced down the streets, out

through the city gates, through forests and fields, on and on.

One morning Karen danced across a lonely heath and came upon a little cottage where a carpenter lived. "Please, save me!" she shouted. "Cut off my feet and the shoes with them." The carpenter did as he was asked and the red shoes danced away by themselves. Now the carpenter was a kind man and he made Karen a pair of wooden feet. They were not as good as real ones, but she quickly got used to them.

A priest in a nearby village gave Karen a job as his housekeeper. She worked hard and said her prayers every night before she went to bed. But each time she tried to enter the church the red shoes appeared and danced in front of the door and would not let her pass.

Then, one morning as Karen was working, she said to herself out loud, "How I wish I had not become so vain. I should never have made my mother buy me those red shoes." Then an angel of God appeared. She carried Karen into the church and gave her back her own feet. It was a miracle and now Karen knew that God had forgiven her for her vanity.